About the Author

I started writing little stories after my father passed. He was an avid gardener, and he and my mother always put food out for the birds and carefully tended a garden of flowers. The stories helped me remember him, and as I wrote them, I was transported to my childhood, ignoring most of what he taught me as I trampled the flower beds playing football. The morning songs of birds and the beauty of nature are often taken for granted, much like the time we have left with our loved ones; so always take a few moments, just for yourself.

The Garden

John Maxwell

The Garden

Olympia Publishers
London

www.olympiapublishers.com
OLYMPIA PAPERBACK EDITION

Copyright © John Maxwell 2023

The right of John Maxwell to be identified as author of
this work has been asserted in accordance with sections 77 and 78 of
the Copyright, Designs and Patents Act 1988.

All Rights Reserved

No reproduction, copy or transmission of this publication
may be made without written permission.
No paragraph of this publication may be reproduced,
copied or transmitted save with the written permission of the publisher,
or in accordance with the provisions
of the Copyright Act 1956 (as amended).

Any person who commits any unauthorised act in relation to
this publication may be liable to criminal
prosecution and civil claims for damage.

A CIP catalogue record for this title is
available from the British Library.

ISBN: 978-1-80439-035-1

This is a work of fiction.
Names, characters, places and incidents originate from the writer's
imagination. Any resemblance to actual persons, living or dead, is
purely coincidental.

First Published in 2023

Olympia Publishers
Tallis House
2 Tallis Street
London
EC4Y 0AB

Printed in Great Britain

Dedication

For my father, whom I will never forget and my mother, may I never take for granted.

Acknowledgements

Thank you to my mum, without your patience, this would have been impossible.

The Garden

Often we are guilty of looking at the world from an all too human perspective. While we bustle through our daily lives, we rarely consider the lives of the smaller creatures that share our homes with us. A garden is its history, a sum of all its stories. Occurrences unremarkable to us which still hold value to those that experienced them. A garden may represent serenity to you, but to others it is less kind. It is good to remember this and be kind to all creatures; for we are more alike than we may realise.

Onana

(Of Spiders)

Onana never knew her mother. She was born with three hundred others in a spindly tree on the outskirts of a wood in early spring. Though she was born in a huge family, she didn't feel any kinship. She spent a few days with her many siblings after moulting her egg sac, growing bigger and stronger in the centre of the writhing mass of yellow spiders. She felt safe in the nest but also grew irritated at the constant scratching and shuffling of her peers.

Her mother had died a few weeks before Onana had hatched, and Onana in turn never gave her any thought. It seemed to Onana that the world had come into existence with her, perhaps even because of her, and she was eager to explore this new awakening. All this is not to say that Onana is a proud spider, just at her early age she had a lot to learn about the world she lived in.

Just as soon as Onana grew hungry, she deemed the time was right. She wriggled and clambered between and around her siblings, and she began to climb the thin spindly tree that had been her home. Higher and higher she climbed at a deliberate pace, her eight eyes ever watchful for dangers; though in truth, six of them were almost blind. She blinked them over and over, but through these she could barely see.

The wind rattled the frail branches and Onana clung with all her legs desperately. Being unfamiliar with the wind, she feared that cold and dreadful force and in these moments was terrified its wailing would never end; but of course, it did. When the wind abated, she again climbed onwards; uncertain as to why or to where, she just knew in her hearts that this was the way. But when she reached the top, she sat still for a while, confused as how to proceed. She looked left; she looked right, but none of her siblings could be seen. So, she sat and she waited, watching the world for inspiration; and what a strange world it was.

As she pondered her next move, she cleaned her fangs with her front legs, this helped her fight the anxiety of the immediate future. She scratched her head where it itched and felt quietly pleased with herself; freedom was good, if a little confusing. Being away from her siblings was a relief, though she wondered what they were all doing and then began to worry, for what if they were doing better than her? Maybe they knew what to do from here. Had she made a mistake? Missed something obvious? She considered going back down to the nest; but then, she was hungry and there was no food down there. She looked about for something to eat, but the branches were empty of anything that looked like food.

It was the early spring and Onana became cold and downcast in the wet morning air. She remained there on her perch, anxiously cleaning herself as the sun grew in strength; as her surroundings transformed, her eyes widened as she beheld for the first time many wonders for which she had no words. As the gloom faded, the fantastic intensity of spring came to the fore. The feeling of warmth on her back, her legs seemed to throb with energy, and she felt a smile cross her face as hope rekindled in her hearts. She stretched laboriously and yawned, her fangs clicking as her mouth closed. She passed the time listening to the lilting songs of other animals, seemingly joyous to be alive.

Finally, she saw out of the corner of her blurry sixth eye, a sibling climbing a parallel branch. Thrilled that she was not the only one to leave the nest; she watched as he reached the end of his branch and then stood perplexed. She noticed him, looking at her and quickly looked away, washing her fangs until he turned again. She noticed other spiders were making their way up to the other branches and were now reaching the top. She felt hunger gnaw angrily, and she shifted her weight impatiently. She noticed with horror as a sister was picked off by a giant winged monster. What was that flying feathered beast? What was this world of wondrous beauty that dealt out death with impunity? She squirmed as she cast her eyes around her for other beasts. What harm could any of them have caused, or could cause, small as they were?

A slight scratch she heard from below and she fixed her senses upon it. Not far beneath her branch, she saw it; stealthily and cruelly another spider, much larger than herself, was creeping ever closer. Its fangs seemed gigantic to her, the eyes devoid of warmth; this was no friend and its intent was nothing short of murder. But how could she escape? She couldn't evade such a creature and could climb no higher! She knew she had to pretend she had not seen it, or it would be upon her in no time. She began to panic as she felt and heard each leg move ever closer, one by one. At last she had an idea! A desperate ploy that could only be better than the jaws of the beast!

She quickly wove simple threads together, throwing them out into the morning air as the spider below began to quicken its pace. She glimpsed a sister twist in the agony of another spider's fangs and as the lethal evil that hungered for her flesh clambered at speed and now, she could see, smell and hear it, and this was it. She had no choice, it was now or never, and so she, herself, leapt! She jumped off the branch, with naught but a tiny bag of silk, that she felt the leaping menace behind her swipe nothing but air! Terrified but triumphant, she evaded her foe, and now, she feared she would fall like a stone to the floor, but then she felt herself being swept up and away as the wind took her parachute! She shook her legs and jeered at the disappointed spider, she which watched her disappointedly fade into nothing. She shivered with relief as she drifted up and away from the killing fields below.

The wind took Onana far away from the forest in which she was born. High above the trees, she travelled in style, seemingly safe from the winged terrors and cruel spiders that haunted the forest. As the forest of her birth faded into the distance, Onana found herself losing altitude and drifted lower and lower before landing roughly; she tucked her legs in and bouncing once, twice and then a third time before rolling gently in the grass.

She sat dazed a moment or two, before she gained her senses and began to climb an inviting plant stem. She would not know it, but she had landed in our garden, a garden with many flowerbeds waiting to bloom and one owner who would look upon her with friendly eyes; though not all that lived there would be as understanding.

This time Onana did not climb to the top, for she was tired and starving and she wanted to settle. She climbed half way up, and glanced about carefully. Yes, this was the spot. She wove a long strand of silk and cast it across at the next plant a foot away. It missed its mark, and she grumbled miserably to herself as she drew it back and recast it. It missed again and she cursed her luck under her breath and drew it back and recast it. Third time the charm, it stuck to a twig, and so, she began to spin another silk line and took it across the original line. She, then, lowered herself on a thread and formed a large silk triangle as the base for her web.

Over the course of the next hour, she built her first web. It was by no means her best work, and in time she would scoff at a web as primitive as this, but for now it would do. She walked across it, meticulously altering areas she could see were clearly a mess and testing her lines, and finally content, she placed herself proudly upon the centre. Now she would sleep and wait.

People often think spiders possess great patience, but this is not true. Onana was a spider that grew bored and anxious quickly, and fortunately for her; she fell fast asleep. Afternoon turned to evening as she slept in her web, dreaming of small flying insects, juicy, fat and blind; flying aimlessly into her web.

She woke with a start and her senses were screaming at her! There! Look! There! The web still gently shook as Onana raced towards the gnat that had stuck in her web. Though she had never done this before; she knew exactly what needed to be done. She greedily pierced it with her fangs and wrapped it up, though she could barely wait for her meal to be ready. As soon as it was she feasted, joyfully slurping it down. Triumphantly, she returned to the centre of her web and her hunting skills now vindicated, she fell back in deep slumber. Such a good spot she had found, she was fortunate enough to repeat this scene twice more, and she felt delightfully full and pleased with herself.

Morning came with light dew hanging on her web; she impatiently waited for it to dry and then gave up. She ate her web, unaware herself as to why, but it seemed the right thing to do. Then she built another one, this one slightly better than her first attempt, she noticed with pleasure. Onana again sat in the centre of her web, assured that today would be a very good day indeed. She napped gently after her web weaving, dreaming pleasantly of more of the gnats that had sated her hunger.

Onana awoke with alarm bells ringing from all quarters. Her web was smashed asunder and she found herself clinging to a giant of a creature that swatted in a panic at the silk it had disturbed. Giant did not adequately describe the size of this beast. The spider before had been many times larger than her and the feathered menace many times of that. This creature was as big as some trees, and it bellowed and shrieked as it thundered about. The creature stood on two legs and in a bizarre turn of events seemed to fear Onana, who in turn screamed back at the beast as she desperately abseiled down from this mysterious danger. The strange creature thundered off into the distance and it was all Onana could do to muse over the situation as she caught her breath. Her hearts pounded as she struggled back to the safety of the undergrowth.

Her web was gone, a few strands hung loosely here and there. Onana waited a while, checking the creature did not return, before eating them and decided it best to move on. Creatures like that might pass by again and she wanted nothing more than to avoid such an encounter.

Onana didn't wander far, for she found a convenient ornate gate of painted metal and within its large gaps, she carefully set a web. She decided here that no longer would she sit in the centre of her web, but remain on the outskirts, a hooked leg touching a strand to alarm her of any activity. But no activity came that day; the next day she ate her web, remade it and waited. Again, nothing came, so the next day she ate up her web and set off again, this time hungrily crawling up the trunk of a cherry tree.

The cherry tree's flowers were just in bloom and the fragrance was sweet and welcoming. It was here she wove her first truly perfect web amongst the eaves. The spot was a good one and Onana caught a variety of insects and flies that helped her reach adulthood.

It was here that Onana began to sing; not every spider likes to sing but Onana certainly did. She had to make up her songs, and so, she sang of the things she knew, of the monsters that she had seen and the journey she had taken; but mostly she sang of the lovely juicy insects she caught.

As the spring turned to summer, Onana lived peacefully amongst the eaves of the cherry tree; every morning going about her routine of recycling her web and building one afresh, then waiting at the side for her daily catches. She was large for her kind, so abundant were the gnats, flies and other unfortunates and had formed her own perspective on life and death in the garden. She understood now that there were two kinds of beast upon the planet, predator and prey; and that one can quite easily slip from one category into the other, so you must always be vigilant. She had observed spiders bigger than herself get overconfident and place their webs in foolish spots, becoming too visible. She had watched as they had been swiftly taken by the feathered monsters that hunt so tenaciously at dawn and dusk. She sang songs about them every day, to learn from their fate or else to share it. That would never be her, Onana swore to herself as she sang, for she would stay out of sight, with one clawed leg upon her web, out of the sight of those monsters.

As time passed, a wider variety of creatures began to find their ways into her web. Mainly beetles and flying ants, and these poor creatures Onana wrapped up with ease, but two occasions would stick with her for her whole life. For every different creature Onana ate, she would make into a song, describing their appearance and taste; she would sing these songs when she caught them, and also when the times were lean to keep her spirits up.

The first unusual encounter was announced by a great and angry buzzing. She heard it long before it crashed into her net. When she saw it coming, she was shocked that such a creature could fly. She marvelled at its blasé inelegance in the air, rising and falling turbulently as it struggled against its own weight. As it got closer, she noticed how fuzzy and furry it really was, black with a gold and white band around its middle. How strange, she pondered, all the creatures that live in this world. It never really looked like it would hit her web, and even if it did, Onana thought it would surely crash straight on through.

But for a reason that Onana could never fathom, the creature suddenly buzzed upwards and upwards, seemingly drunk on the perfume of the cherry tree! Up and up and up and crash! It struck the very centre of her web, and she thought it had indeed passed straight through when suddenly the web sprang back, with furry creature tangled in the centre! The web bounced and bounced as she made her way cautiously to her prey. Lucky she did, for she noticed a long sharp sting and two strong jaws gnashing and flailing. She pondered at length how to get closer to the creature when it spoke out to her!

It spoke of many things and Onana, having never been spoken to, by anything, listened. Puzzled, and more than a little wary, Onana spoke back to the creature, which called itself a Bee. She told it her stories as it wriggled and writhed, and she began to enjoy its company. After a while, she began to feel more than a little sorry for the bee, so obviously terrified and she cut him loose and carefully ate the strands of web so he could again fly. The bee was flinched in terror as she carefully moved around him, but when she was finished, opened his eyes and buzzed his wings in delight. He thanked Onana for her mercy and praised her beauty and wisdom, words Onana would quickly put into her song about this encounter.

Onana watched the bee fly off, wishing him well but knowing in her hearts that he would surely buzz clumsily into another spider's web; another spider who might be less merciful. She felt a spasm of hunger and began to regret her decision, though when a fly soon became entangled, she knew she had done the right thing.

Not too long after, a surprising thing happened. She saw her friend, the bee, returning to her. He landed nearby, and with a quick thank you, put a glob of thick yellow liquid near her. He explained that he didn't have much with which to thank her, but to his kind this was their greatest treasure. Almost embarrassed, he flew off again. Onana looked at the strange liquid. Curious as to what it was; she dipped a claw and found it sticky. She tasted the liquid, and my goodness, she had never experienced anything like it. Deliciously sweet and fragrant! She greedily consumed it all and felt this strange energy rushing through her. She decided she would remake her whole web again right now.

From there on, every time Onana saw a bee, she would call out to them, as she missed the conversation, but on each occasion the bee would eye her distrustfully and fly away. She hoped her friend was alive still, but would never hear of him again.

The second occasion of note was another buzzing creature, though slimmer in size and more dangerous in its appearance. Summer was nearly over and the garden in which Onana lived smelled strongly of the fermenting apples that had dropped from the orchard nearby. This creature could fly well, Onana observed; with a thin body and an angry expression, it had a real essence of lethality about it. It hovered close to her web, and for no reason, attacked! It launched itself at Onana, who with one foot on her web was startled into action and raced across her web. The creature followed her through the air its angry stinger wet with venom came dangerously close! It struck at her again and its abdomen got caught in the web!

The creature cursed Onana, wriggled about furiously, calling her a coward and swearing an oath that it would kill her yet! Onana tilted her head to the side, watching as the creature got more entangled as it wriggled about. As she could understand it, she tried to talk to the angry creature, but all she received were taunts and insults. Onana was mystified by the furious hate this creature seemed to bear for her and everything around her, even the beautiful cherry tree. Onana walked to the side of her web determined to leave her wicked guest to hang in her web all day until it gets tired, and maybe she could have a civil conversation with it. She was also quite scared of him to be truthful. She, in time, learnt that it called itself a wasp, and the wasp kept swearing and taunting her for the entire time it was in her web. Onana wondered at how a creature could be so hateful. On and on, it shouted vicious nasties, until eventually Onana could take no more.

Onana shouted back at the wasp after a particularly unpleasant comment about her eyes; and she roared into action and attacked the wicked wasp with a fury. She leapt atop the wasp and bit him, injecting him with her venom. The wasp in its last hateful moments somehow bit back and bit half of one of her left legs off. Onana screamed in agony and shuffled away from the wasp, whose breath was ragged but was laughing at her. It laughed and it laughed, defiant to the end. Onana cried and cried long after the wasp had grown still. She cradled her leg which hurt so badly. Never before had she experienced anything so cruel. She wept as she ate the hateful creature; she wept as she repaired her ruined web. Onana thought she might just weep forever.

Onana's leg healed over but never regrew as she vaguely hoped it might. That incident scarred Onana forever, and not just her body. The songs she sang became more regretful and sad; she sang songs of the wasp and her lost leg more than her happy songs, for the experience was forever in her thoughts. As summer passed into autumn, she felt the cold, more strongly than ever; and she decided to leave the cherry tree that had been her home for most of her life. Before she left she looked back at her tree and smiled wistfully, before turning her back on it never to return.

Onana was cold, so she followed the warmth. The old house nearby offered light and heat, so Onana climbed up to a window and looked in; a huge fire crackled merrily in a hearth and she found its flames somewhat comforting. She could see two gargantuan figures in armchairs close to the fires, one of which was surely the creature that broke her web. She sang her song to remind her of the experience and decided to be cautious. She crept into the house as only a spider can, through secret spaces humans are too large to notice but to a spider are great caves. She set herself up high in a corner near the fire and snugly slept through the night. This was the life, Onana reasoned, other creatures shall surely follow here and I will not grow hungry.

In the night Onana decorated her corner with a beautiful web, even after losing half a leg she could still weave perfectly. She looked over at it and settled down into a deep sleep.

She awoke to the loudest sound she had ever heard, such a great screeching and bellowing. It was that strange creature again! Pointing at Onana as it jumped up and down on one spot making unearthly sounds the whole time. Onana saw in its eyes the same fear as the creatures she caught, and could not fathom what threat she could possibly pose to this beast.

The other one came scuttling into the room alarmed. It looked to where the crazy one was pointing, and it rolled its huge eyes and sighed as it shook its massive head. It muttered words that Onana could not understand as it grabbed for some paper and a cup. Onana cowered in her corner and screamed rooted in terror as the creature came closer and closer, before suddenly she was trapped herself! She scuttled this way and that but kept hitting a solid invisible barrier on all sides. Realising she was trapped; she stopped scuttling and scratching at her chamber, and she just cried and cried in terror and sadness. She could think of no songs to lift her hearts. Her world shifted and swayed and she was thrown from side to side as the creature moved with her. She felt sick with fear and dizzy from the experience. Finally, she saw the outside world appear, and she was set down on a pebbly path. She ran as fast as she could, away from the house, vowing never to return!

At the edge of her path, Onana stopped to catch her breath; she decided to make a long song about the house and the two-legged creatures so that she would remember never to return, but as she sat pondering this new song, a great shadow appeared overhead and a deadly swooshing sound as something huge descended from above. Onana looked up confused and saw a great winged beast! Before she could even think to run, she felt its beak grab her and her whole world turned to darkness.

Titus

(Of Cats)

My sister thinks I sleep a lot, even for a cat. The truth is I mostly pretend to sleep because, and I am sorry to brag, but I am something of a thinker. The world I live in can be quite confusing, so I mostly ponder it and the behaviours of the creatures I live with, trying to make sense of it all. Sometimes yes, I admit it, this leads me to fall asleep, and often, I forget what I was thinking about too. I raise myself and slowly stretch, arching my back and flexing my claws and I plod at my own pace downstairs for some food. My sister has gone out again, I notice with some relief; she can be quite difficult and judgemental. Always looking to come in or go out. It is a constant back in, back out, back in again and back out again, which to me it seems quite exhausting. There's nothing really out there to do or see, and mostly it is quite cold or wet. I don't like the rain myself, for nothing looks sadder than a wet cat in my eyes; although this empty bowl I have arrived at comes close.

Into the living room I go to rouse one of my human friends. I barge the door open with more strength than I had intended, and it rattles against some furniture. They notice me with delight and a cacophony of kind words fall upon me. I take these compliments with a certain bored grace. Yes, that's right, yes, it's true; I am indeed a good and a handsome cat. This isn't what I came for, so I blink up at them with bored eyes and watch them patiently. They sit up and stare back slowly, blinking their eyes stupidly at me. Damn it, I curse as I feel myself slowly blinking back at them. This goes on for a short while, and as they are not getting the hint, I dig my claws in the carpet and scratch and stretch. Disappointed sounds from the sofa and I inwardly smile. Yes, yes, I am sorry that was wrong of me, never again, yes, now give me food. You're the ones that keep it out of my reach; if I could, I'd happily get it myself. One of them stands up and I look at him expectantly.

He picks me up and gives me a cuddle which though I enjoy, this is not what I am here for. I wriggle and writhe, and he puts me down. He opens the front door for me, and I stare up at him irritated. It's like he doesn't even know me. I am not Tanit, she's undoubtedly at another door now wanting to come back in before wanting to go back out again, but I am not her. These humans I think viciously, they have all the power, but really, they aren't that bright. I sit myself down and continue to stare at him with bored, impatient eyes. Yes, that's right, close the door, obviously I do not want to go outside. I swear we go through this every day, but he does not learn. I meow at him, trying to speak his strange language. He meows back at me and I know that is not what I sound like. Slightly insulted, I scuttle to the kitchen, turning occasionally to make sure he gets the hint. Good yes, he is following me.

To speed things up, I pace between the empty food bowls and the cupboard where I know the food is kept, meowing at him and occasionally nuzzling his feet. He likes that a lot and tells me how wonderful I am as he finally opens the cupboard to get me some food. A voice from the other room and he turns, about to abandon his duty, so I put myself between him and the voice and meow again. Yes, that's right, me now, whatever is going on in there, later. I feel it is important to be firm sometimes; that you need to lead your humans and take charge, or else nothing would ever get done.

At last the food is in the bowl, and he puts it down accordingly. He leaves the kitchen and I eat my fill; now to climb back up the stairs. I clamber somewhat slower than I came down if I am honest, for I have eaten more than I had originally intended. I jump back on this month's preferred bed, I do like to change my scenery every month, I find it helps the thought process. As I curl myself up, I hear a door open and my sister, Tanit, scuttling back into the house; she is really so predictable, I think to myself.

Now it is time to consider the charade I just had to go through with the human; was there some way I could have acted to get my point across quicker? I like to go over these things for there is always room for improvement, and tomorrow would likely be a similar day for me. Satisfied that the issue was with him rather than me, I find myself falling inexorably into a deep sleep.

Fiske and Hilde

(Of Birds)

Fiske and Hilde are bullfinches. The male bullfinch (as in Fiske's case) announces its arrival with a shock of colour, for its head and chest are a startling red. Their backs are grey and their wings black. Their heads are bulky yet small, "bullish", if you will. They are about five inches tall and are in shape like a plump, stout robin. The female closely resembles the male in shape but neither in colour nor in size; for she is slightly smaller, and where he is red; she is pale brown. Bullfinches have a quiet piping song that more often than not is drowned out by the din of other, noisier birds.

We pick up the story of Fiske and Hilde just after they first met each other. Both born in spring the previous year, they are now just shy of a year old and each has responded to the others songs; which has led to this encounter on the garden floor. Fiske circles Hilde slowly, cooing softly to her; Hilde lowers her head bashfully and scrapes a foot back and forth on the ground. Fiske flutters off quickly, and for a minute; Hilde looks disappointed and more than a little confused. Barely a minute passes when with a flutter of black wings and a flash of brilliant red, Fiske returns with twigs in his beak. He circles her again, his song muffled by the twigs; then they fly off together and make a home in a nearby tree.

A month passes and it is finally spring; they have built a nest from twigs and moss, and in this nest, Fiske sits gently atop four pale blue eggs. Hilde is out searching for food and luckily, in this garden a man puts feeders out filled with seeds and fat. She notices a spider on the path and with a flutter of wings, swoops and devours it. She flies to a nearby branch and eyes the feeders warily for dangers. She remembers a time not long ago when she saw a cat stroll casually through the garden. It stalked through the grass on four legs, with jet black fur and piercing eyes of yellowy green; it had looked her way and she had felt its menace. There were some birds in the garden that took this threat lightly, that flew from branch to ground with barely a glance. She had seen first-hand what happens to them and vowed it would not happen to her. With no visible threats, she took off and landed on the feeder; she fed on the sunflower seeds, then back to the nest so that Fiske could feed.

Fiske was markedly different to Hilde, not only in appearance but in nature. He was as confident in nature as he was loud in colour and had little time for Hilde's cautiousness. He too had seen the cat, but he noticed that it was well fed, lazy and mostly absent. When it was visible, it was rarely awake and it mostly groomed itself or patrolled the garden before going back inside. He made for the feeder immediately and lingered longer than Hilde would, taking joy in the feeling of food in his mouth and sunshine on his wings. Sated for now, he returned to the nest.

Spring was cold. Though winter had passed, it would not be shaken off entirely; nights were still long and mornings were frosty. Hilde and Fiske fed often, thankful for the bounty available at the feeders as they kept their eggs warm. They waited impatiently for their eggs to hatch and soon enough, they did.

They were noisy little chicks; always hungry and cold. They huddled together for warmth and cried out ceaselessly for food. Hilde and Fiske fed nearly non-stop throughout the days, keeping their young well fed before sleeping deep when the sun went down. The chicks grew fast, as well-fed chicks do. They began to move around more in the nest, eager to learn more about the world that surrounded it. The call of the chicks was heard by all in the garden, but not all that heard these sounds were friendly.

One morning, while Fiske was out feeding, he heard a panicked call; a cry of anguish and terror. He dropped the seed he was about to eat and rushed for the nest. Hilde was attacking a magpie, screeching at it as she flapped and dived around it, desperately trying to dissuade the much larger bird. The magpie had a mad and greedy glint to its eye and it did not heed Hilde's threats. Fiske dove for the magpie and crashed into its wing. The magpie cried out in pain as it fell from the branch. It immediately fluttered back up and eyed the dazed Fiske angrily. Fiske groggily dodged a dangerous peck as Hilde nipped at the exposed wing of the magpie before veering out of range. The magpie turned menacingly back towards Hilde who fluttered just out of range, trying to tempt the magpie away from the nest. The magpie croaked at maliciously as it hopped forward, leaning in and grabbing a chick with its wicked beak. The chick squeaked in terror as the magpie took to flight, and just like that a chick was gone.

Hilde and Fiske were devastated, but they could not pause in grief; life must go on with three remaining chicks to feed. As time passed, they grew larger still and had started to grow the feathers for flight. They bounced with energy now, with spring in full ascendency and it wouldn't be long before they were ready to leave the nest themselves. Hilde and Fiske were a bit thinner than they had been, all the energy of feeding their chicks had taken its toll, but finally, the chicks were ready to fly. Fiske and Hilde watched with joy as they took flight.

A little clumsily they took to the air and followed Fiske to the feeder. One of the chicks in particular seemed to be having a hard time of it. What had started so well quickly turned for the worse. She muddled herself in flight, and she spiralled down and hit the ground with a thud. She called out in a panic as she fluttered and hopped about amongst the grass. Fiske and Hilde called out, desperately encouraging her. Her instincts told her something was wrong and she lost herself in panic. Fiske landed nearby and tried to calm and set her straight again. She paused and seemed to compose herself, and Fiske took to the air in demonstration. She fluttered and flapped, and she rose in the air. Out of the undergrowth there was a streak of black as something hurtled towards them. The black streak leapt and batted the chick out of the air. Hilde screeched out in grief as she saw her nightmare come to life. The chick flapped in panic and pain and called out in desperation, trying to escape the cat. Suddenly pinned to the floor, Fiske and Hilde watched as jaws clamped on the chick's wing. Fiske dove at the cat, which dropped the chick obligingly as it twisted and jumped to swipe at him murderously. He veered up and away, barely dodging the needle like claws that swished through the air. The chick flapped on the floor trying to take off, but her wing was broken. It hung limply at her side as she bleated desperately at Hilde in horror. Hilde cried out as the cat clamped its mouth around her tiny body and watched as her eye slowly closed, never to open again.

Alas again, for the bullfinches, life had to go on. Though Fiske and Hilde felt their hearts were broken, they went on. The other two chicks were ready now to leave, and one morning they did. With no ceremony they took off, looking for mates and nests of their own.

The nest was quiet with only Fiske and Hilde, though after a few weeks passed, there were five more eggs for them to warm. With summer blooming and food aplenty, Fiske and Hilde regained their strength, but they were concerned. Where four of their eggs were warm, one was cool. When four of their eggs began to crack and hatch, one did not. Four chicks emerged strong and healthy, but one did not. The day turned to night, the night back to day, but the passing of sun and moon brought no change to the fifth egg. In the morning light Hilde and Fiske looked sadly at the egg in silence; finally, Fiske shuffled towards it and with rolled it from the nest. The pale blue egg fell swiftly and cracked on impact. A twisted, lifeless form was finally revealed; tragically this chick had been dead for days. Hilde and Fiske went about their business that day with heavy hearts. They tried to ignore the sight below and were almost relieved the next day when they awoke to find it gone.

The weather in summer can be temperamental, and after a few searing hot days the weather changed. A storm, the likes of which neither Fiske nor Hilde had experienced, broke out and a lashing rain began to fall during an afternoon. Water dripped through the branches and the nest was soaking. Though they huddled over their four chicks, it was impossible to keep them warm and dry. The storm continued on through to the night and the young chicks shivered. Fiske and Hilde clutched each other tight as the wind shook the branches and thunder and lightning shattered the night sky. The nest fell into a sort of wakeful sleep, exhaustion replacing fear as the storm finally broke deep in the night.

The sun rose to expose a scene of chaos. A nearby tree had been uprooted and lay fallen where it had crashed down, strewn across the garden path. The flowers had been broken by the wind; their petals littered the grass in patches of colour. The bullfinches awoke stiff and finally dry. They stretched and tried to shake the nightmares of the storm away. Hilde cried out in surprise. Fiske turned and the extent of the tragedy was revealed. Two chicks yet remained alive and two had succumbed to the storm. Was it the cold or the damp that had taken their lives, or perhaps the terror of the storm? All that mattered is that the night had taken them and now there was little to do but to remove them from the nest and again go on. Fiske shuffled them out of the nest with immeasurable grief in his heart as Hilde went off to the feeder.

Again, they woke next morning to find their little

bodies removed by the night creatures, probably one of the foxes that occasionally woke them with their mating calls.

There is little more to add to their tale, so we will leave them here. The two chicks made it to adulthood and left the nest without further incident, and Hilde and Fiske would not lay more eggs that year. The life of a bird is one of constant endeavour and hardship, and in this way, Fiske and Hilde lived the remainder of their years.

Olwen

(Of Mice)

Olwen woke in confusion. She lay on her side with a great pain in her ribs and numbness in her legs. She blinked her large black eyes and squinted at the darkness. She could see nothing. She sniffed the air and memory rushed back immediately. Out of nowhere in the dark, she recalled the sound of an animal rushing; the agony of claws and being carried in a monster's mouth.

Something told her she needed to remain completely still, and she focused on this as she struggled to control her ragged breathing. A terrifying yowl split the air and Olwen could make out bright yellow eyes in the night.
Another long, drawn out yowl and Olwen felt rising panic. To stay here seemed certain death. She flew off in the direction she was facing, with no idea where she was headed in the darkness. She felt certain she could make it if she just kept running; somewhere, anywhere that was not here would do. She could hear the beast with yellow eyes swiping at her barely a breath behind as they streaked across the garden desperately. She took a paw to the side and crashed to the floor, pinned beneath it. Again, the feeling of pointy teeth in her side; Her vision swam and once again the darkness took her.

She awoke in the jaws of the beast. Carried in the warm, wet mouth Olwen again struggled to get her bearings. She knew that to struggle would cause the cat to bite hard and that would be the end of her. She thought of her family, most likely eating seeds and insects and completely oblivious to her plight; she willed herself to make it through this and return to them. Meanwhile, the beast carried her almost tenderly in its jaws. With every step it took, Olwen found herself wincing in pain, however, other than bruising, she felt no lasting damage. The cat jumped and leapt through a window into the big house.

The environment here was different; Olwen felt a great stillness in the air, and the house was completely silent. The smell was overpowering. The two cats and the two humans that lived here and the food they ate and the food they threw away. If not for the cats, Olwen and her people would have been quite happy here and could live quite undetected from the clumsy humans.

Life is cruel to wood mice, Olwen thought, as she hung limp in the cat's mouth. These owls and cats hold great advantage over them. Claws, teeth, talons and beaks multiplied by a size and weight advantage. If she could deliver a bite, she was determined to do so, for she too had teeth. A reminder that Olwen, too, was life and her life had meaning; if only to her kind.

With a thud she was dropped to the floor. There was absolute darkness in this room, and though she heard a rustling of the two humans and could smell their den, it was apparent that they were asleep. Strange creatures indeed, that sleep when the air is coolest and awaken to the wicked sun. A great yowl cuts the air again.

The silence grew heavier as the humans woke startled. Another yowl cut the air. The humans emitted some grumbling sounds as they sat up and blinked into the darkness. Another long yowl, more insistent this time. Huge feet hit the floor as one of the humans rose, as tall as a tree, it thudded across the room. Olwen tensed expecting one of those giant feet to crush her, but luckily, it landed mere inches away.

A great light shattered the darkness, the room bathed in a blinding mysterious light that permeated all corners and brought a wince to every living being in that room. Olwen finally saw the cat that had caught her, that great black monster recoiling momentarily from the glaring light.

A strange sound escaped the human as its eyes fell upon Olwen, prone on the floor. Are mice really this repulsive to all creatures? Olwen thought bitterly. Are we born into this world to be bitten and gored, crushed and abhorred? What did we ever do to deserve this, our great crime of survival?

She felt the cat swish its tail and pounce, and at the last moment, Olwen darted away and took refuge in a shoe. She pushed herself deep into the end and felt the cat's paw scrabbling away, but she made herself small and remained tantalisingly out of reach.

Here, Olwen went over her options. To leave seemed certain death, but she could not stay here forever either. Olwen decided that if she were to die, she would rather die here in the shoe than make her body a gift or a meal. She did not want to die that way, better to stay here and hope the cat grew tired and gave up.

She could see the cat nearby, circling furiously. Suddenly, she felt something huge land on her hiding place and all light was extinguished. Her world shifted as she was hoisted off the ground and she heard the deep steady voice of the human; was it speaking to her?

She was bounced and rattled with every huge step as the human carried her away. Was this the end? Would she be crushed or eaten whole, or to be given to the cat that no doubt followed eagerly in the human's wake.

A strange sound of a door opening and closing gently, and though she was wrapped and trapped in the shoe, she could smell the night air. She felt the show being turned upside down and she rolled over upright again. The blanket removed, she could taste the night air again. The soft sounds of the human seemed to encourage her, and she decided that even if this were a trap, best to try, and without ceremony she raced and bounded as fast as she could from the shoe. Every breath hurt from her bruised ribs, and her legs were stiff and sore, but she ran as best as she could until she found the undergrowth.

She looked back at the human and tentatively smiled as he murmured more encouragement. Behind him she saw the cat glaring murderously in the window, locked inside for at least this night. She turned and sniffed the air. "This way," she muttered and began her short trip home. She desperately needed a rest and after all, she now had quite the story to tell.

Khnni

(Of Owls)

I am night stalker; I am death. The slightest breeze hides my beating wings as I hunt throughout the night. Motionless and vigilant I wait, poised atop this branch in anticipation. My claws are like daggers, my beak a razors edge; all that know me live in fear. This is my garden and the night belongs to me. In the cover of darkness, my prey feels secure, as though I am can't hear nor see them. This mistake will cost them many lives, for I am hidden slaughter, just waiting to be unleashed.

I listen carefully with my watch barely begun, the scene below is illuminated by the dappled moonlight, but I mainly listen. I fancy I can hear the step of every insect, the beating heart of every mouse. They are undoubtedly nearby but hidden, these impetuous desperate creatures. Their need to keep moving and searching would soon enough expose them and then they will be mine. Already I hear a gentle rustle, a slight crinkle of a tiny paw upon a leaf. My head swivels and my pupils dilate even further. I fix on its location as a light gust of wind rattles through the wintry trees. I take to the air soundlessly. The prey never suspects me, never realises I am near. It does not react until my pierce its flesh and lift it from the grass. I can now feel as well as hear the rapid heartbeat of the creature, writhing in agony and terror before quickly, mercifully, the life extinguishes and the mouse grows still. I land in the trees and devour it quickly, even now watchful for the next.

My hunger is not sated; I seek at least two more simple delicacies before my watch is ended. What will it be I wonder? Mouse again? Perhaps a vole? Maybe a shrew? Or something unusual? A bat or a careless bird? Out of the safety of its nest? That would be a treat, as one can grow bored of the taste of rodent. Yet these are rare occurrences indeed, for most in the garden are now old enough to know I lurk in the shadows. I am always watching, nothing that moves below is hidden from me.

The moon is now at its highest. Today it is colossal, its cold light now shines down upon me completely. I see below my shadow upon the ground, I spread my wings and marvel at my power. I imagine my prey below me, awestruck at my beauty and frozen in terror. I listen, but I hear nothing. I look up at the moon and I screech my name to it! "Khnni!" I shriek, staring up expectantly. The moon says nothing. It never does, but I bask in its wondrous glory. I shriek again, and I hear below the terrified movements of a vole that can't bear to hear my name spoken once more. My head swivels, and my gaze fixes upon it! I know where it came from, and I know where it will go! I swoop and glide murderously, and within two seconds, it is mine. I again feel the rapturous joy at the hunt, the dizzying ecstasy of the vole's life dissipating in the crush of my grip. I look to the moon and scream my name again, but as always it just stares on back at me. I gulp down my kill, and I marvel at my talons. I flex them and feel them scratch at the tree bark. Back and forth I scrape them, enjoying the scratch, the feeling and the sound. Scratch, scratch, scratch as I watch the garden below me.

    The moon begins to wane as my watch nears its end. I wait ever patient, as creatures make mistakes around this time. Either following one last scent trail, or scurrying back to their homes, a tired rodent is a vulnerable one. I admit I am impetuous for my kind, and I soundlessly shift my weight and ruffle my feathers in the cold air. I focus more intently on my watch; I close my eyes and concentrate on the sounds around me as a distraction from the cold. I imagine I hear a spider make a kill, and I pretend it calls out in triumph; I picture it, bundle up its victim, enjoying this little reverie.

    I realise I am dozing and jolt myself awake. Covered by my dreaming, I had missed the delicate tip-toeing of feet and a beating heart. Another vole! I focus in on it, confident in the outcome. It pauses, as though aware of me. I jump and I plunge as the vole tries desperately to escape. My pupils dilate as I hear it scurry back towards its den. My talons clench and I almost pull away so sure of my dive, but they clench around nothing! A rare miss; I scold myself for falling asleep, knowing this failure to be its consequence. Furious, I return to my perch and I glance up at the moon, which seems to be judging me silently.

    It is nearly dawn, and I know that my watch has all but ended. Normally, I would go back to my den in the barn, but I feel the need to feed once more; to demonstrate to the moon my prowess. Alas, the dawn begins to break, and I feel myself growing very tired. It hurts, but I must admit defeat. I can almost hear the creatures that no doubt snicker at me from below.

I fly back towards my home, and I see the cat watching me respectfully. I have respect for the cat, from one apex predator to the other, though I know I am more successful. I leave my watch, almost handing the garden over to the cats, for we take turns to terrorise this garden. I screech my name at the cat, "Khnni! Khnni!" The cat watches on with yellow green eyes, I'm never sure who would win if it came down to it, for I am king of the skies and the cat is the lord of the earth.

I arrive in my barn and I am about to settle up and sleep when what was that down in the straw! A rustle and a shuffle of a lost shrew! I descend eagerly and unable to escape, I feel the shrew in my grasp! I squeeze it delightedly as it lets out a high-pitched wail that sounds like my name! "Khnni!" I screech back at the shrew, feeling it die. "Khnni!" I triumphantly screech my name for all to hear as I flutter up to my perch. I tuck my head under my wing and prepare myself for a good day's sleep. It won't be long little creatures, I muse menacingly, before my watch begins again.

Arlo

(Of Hedgehogs)

When take up our story of Arlo at the age of two years old. He is just waking up, but not from a day's sleep, instead from a long hibernation. It is early march, and Arlo is thin and ravenously hungry, he needs to regain the weight he has lost in order to survive the next winter.

    I yawn as I wake groggily from a very deep sleep. I stretch my legs and my claws, and looking down at my skinny tummy, I realise that I may have overslept. I don't think I have ever felt so cold or so hungry, and I wonder how long I have slept for. Perhaps I have missed the whole winter by the smell of the air? Anyway, let's go and investigate.

    I love my burrow; it is normally snug and cosy, although on this evening everything feels cold. I dug most of it myself too, although if I am truly honest, a rabbit did begin the project. I pause at the entrance to my burrow and sniff at the air. "Yep," I sigh, definitely spring. It had been my intention to experience winter this year, as for I have heard it's a most beautiful time of year. I sense no dangers in the air, and I shuffle quickly out of my door and into the undergrowth. I normally hunt for insects, but right now, I will eat more or less anything. Don't judge me; I've slept for many moons.

My menu is arranged by opportunity and I will eat more or less non-stop for the next six hours. First, I smell a yummy slug. I hope it's yellow and fat and long and slimy. I follow its trail anticipating a delicious snack. There, not far away I find it. Black and thick, I munch it down quickly. It doesn't even touch my appetite, for I am feeling voracious tonight. Next a crawling beetle, I hear it scuttling and I smell its trail. I quickly run it down, for I am a fine sprinter, even with my armour. I crunch it and I munch it and I swallow it down. It feels like I haven't even eaten; I am so hungry still.

I shuffle onwards, munching and slurping at everything I come across, it feels so good to eat.

I'm curious to how many moons have passed whilst I slept, although it isn't really important.

What matters is what I found in this bowl! I fancied it might be here for it often is. I bumped into it with my nose before I saw it. A big bowl of milk! It comes from the big house and the creatures inside. I slurp it greedily, until my nose touches the bottom and my tongue can't find any more. I rest sated, that was delicious. I feel much fuller now, so full actually that I don't feel like moving.

I rest here, burping and belching, a paw holding my swollen belly and feeling thankful to the creatures form the house. As I rest, I notice up above me that foolish owl staring at me. He stands as still as stone and shines pale in the moonlight. His oval face is ghostly pale. I know he has been aware of me for a time now, but the period of my life when he could threaten me is at an end. I smile up at him, encouraged by the sneer that takes hold of his face. He looks away, barely able to hide his contempt. I chuckle to myself and slowly move on, happy to be awake and alive, feeling secure in myself; it was not always so.

I was born in a litter of four in the very same burrow I live now; Hoglets, my mother would call us, as we nuzzled at her for milk and warmth. Those early days are mostly forgotten, but shards of memory yet remain. I recall the long lazy days clinging to my mother, at the cusp between sleep and wakefulness; far too small to survive on my own. The soft mumblings and murmurings, the gentle snores from a sibling's dream adding to the cosiness of our burrow. The nights, however, were long and dreadful as mother would leave to hunt and being too small to join her, we had yet to remain.

None of us slept in those long nights during her absence, the silence of night punctuated by the screams of that silly owl. We must be silent, mother always warned before she left, for if we weren't, a fox might come and eat us all. She had described the fox on many occasions. A creature tall and thin with great long teeth and wicked eyes, its tail wreathed in flame! She said that it shone bright in the moonlight, and that a fox's appetite was so great, it could eat ten Hoglets in one sitting and still be wanting.

We never made a sound, not just for fear of the fox. So great was the foreboding, the fear that mother would not return to us ensured we stared out at the night with wide eyes, almost sick with worry. But mother always returned, and we met her with small cries of relief, in some cases a silent tear of gratitude as we nuzzled for milk and warmth once more.

Such times do not last. We grew big and strong on mother's milk, and before too long, it was time for us to follow her outside to hunt. We learnt fast for mother was such a great teacher; she taught us what to eat and what to avoid, which animals could be trusted and which were a threat.

One night the five of us were snuffling along in the night along the trail of a juicy fat slug when I bumped into my brother. I let out a groan and rubbed my snout and was shushed immediately. My mother was frozen with fear, and I felt terror rise within myself. I gasped in shock; there not twenty feet away was the great and wicked fox. Bathed in a pool of moonlight, it groomed its fiery tail. With each lick, long deadly daggers were revealed, and I could see there its cruel claws. It was enormous. Fear gripped me tight. I felt my spines harden and stand on edge. The fox finished its grooming and its ears pricked as it strained for sounds from the night. Its breath steamed in the cold night, and I could just see the wretched beast breathing fire to burn us up! I swear the wicked monster glanced at me with malevolent amusement, before suddenly a great shriek not far away took its attention. It sprang to all fours and loped off into the night. As it disappeared with a swish of its tail, I could finally breathe.

Before too long our family had consumed most of the life in the garden, or so it seemed. We had to go further and further out to keep our bellies full and this led us out of our comfort zone. I now know there are some paths a hedgehog should never take, some areas that are forbidden to us. For there are creatures out there that are beyond our understanding.

We left the garden one waxing moon, the night air chill and silent. I felt great tension as we passed the big house where the strange creatures lived, that was definitely out of bounds. We came to a place where the grass suddenly stopped, where even earth had turned to stone. My mother led the way carefully, snuffling the strange pathway. Her keen eyes stared into the night as she listened and waited. She grunted that we follow and my brothers did, but I lingered here on the grass. One foot on the cold surface, every fibre of my being screamed NO!

My mother turned to admonish or encourage me, but before she could speak, two blinding lights appeared, the eyes of some colossal monstrosity. It raced towards us and it released a terrible sound of raw power. We all stopped and stared in fright. I shut my eyes against the light, but over the din of its terrible belly, I heard the sounds of my mother and my siblings killed. The beast was still, and suddenly, one of the creatures from the house appeared. Heavy footsteps as it came closer to where my family lay dead. It gave a great cry as the massacre was revealed. I whimpered in terror and grief as the creature bent down and scooped me up, but so shocked was I that I closed my eyes. What could I do; anyway, a tiny little hoglet like me in a world of such cruelty? I was carried into house. It was warm in here, and I was placed down near a fire. Milk appeared before me, and though at first I was too shocked and terrified to drink, before too long I found myself desperately guzzling it down.

I do not know how long I stayed in the house, perhaps the passing of a moon, maybe two. All I know is that I became a companion to the black cats that live with the two strange creatures; these cats also hate the fox with a passion. My grief gripped me tightly for so long I had almost lost the desire to live, yet the creatures kept me fed on milk and meat, and the black cats kept me company while time passed.

I was put out in the garden one evening with a bowl of milk beside me. I heard the door to the house slowly close. I looked back and saw the cats and the creatures watching me through the window. Even now, a few years later, I look back at the time with great emotion. Though I will never stop feeling the loss of my mother and my siblings, I am still here. Without the creatures in the house, I would never have survived, so I am thankful to them. I always welcome the company of the black cats, when they occasionally join me in the night, sometimes watching over me while I eat, sometimes sharing the milk that is put out.

These are my thoughts as I pause by the empty bowl, but it is time to move on again. I sniff out the trail of another juicy slug. I follow it greedily humming to myself and I hear noises up ahead of me; "Ah," I say aloud, "the great wicked fox." It sneers at me as it approaches. I smile as I lengthen and straighten my spines, knowing it cannot take me at this age. I back suddenly into him and he cries out with a yelp as I spear him a little. I see one of my cat friends watching from a window in the house, and I try to lance the fox again, this time for the cats. The fox doges and scampers off into the darkness. I smile back at the cat happily before continuing on after that tasty slug. It is good to be alive.

Era

(Of Squirrels)

Era wakes to a freezing dawn; the sun shining weakly and casting a pale light over the garden. She looks out below the tree she nests in, and sees the snowfall from overnight. She shivers, as much from anticipation of the biting snow as from the temperature. It is the last weeks of winter, and she curls her tail around her for warmth and closes her eyes for another few minutes.

The birds are in full voice, and Era knows that she will need to get moving now lest they take all the food from the feeders, which have not been filled in a while. She has barely eaten enough herself recently and she rises slowly, trying vainly to shake off the night's lethargy and ignore her hunger. She runs along the branch, pausing where it meets the trunk of the tree. She surveys the garden for threats, her whiskers twitch and her eyes linger in the shadows; shadows where a cat might hide. There are no telling prints in the snow and seeing nothing suspicious, she scrambles down the trunk and bounds across the snowy garden. She makes straight for the feeder, the cold snow biting her sensitive feet.

She gets to the feeders and scares the flittering birds away with her arrival. She finds them completely empty.

No peanuts today, nor sunflower seeds, once a bountiful cornucopia reduced to rattling cages. There are some balls of suet hanging temptingly. These have, of course, been attacked by the hungry birds, and Era would love to get to them, but they have been put in a type of feeder which seems somehow designed to stop her. The balls are kept tantalisingly behind two cages, and she cannot reach through. She jumps on top of it and tries to find a way in, knowing there must be a trick to it. She struggles on for a minute or so until she huffs in frustration and gives up. Seeing no dangers, she leaves the feeders, and in her hunger decides it is time to dig up some of the acorns she has buried for such a day.

She brushes away the snow and digs quickly in one of her favourite spots, her eyes constantly on the lookout for predators or other squirrels who could be watching jealously from the branches. She gathers up an acorn and is disappointed to find that it has sprouted; this is no good at all she sighs, hungrily discarding the acorn. She digs and rummages further in the ground and pulls out another. Seeing this too had sprouted, she discards it and heads to another spot. Hunger gnaws at her and she starts to panic internally, for what if all her acorns have sprouted?

She brushes the snow away and starts to dig and is alarmed to find the soil here has been disturbed. She digs and rummages, but finds nothing at all. She casts angry eyes up at the branches above, certain that one of the other squirrels had seen her bury her acorns long ago and had stolen her treasure. Hunger stops for no squirrel, and Era goes on to her next spot.

Here she digs, and is pleased the soil is intact. She

digs and she digs but surprisingly finds nothing. She scratches her head puzzled, certain that she had buried them here and cannot understand what has happened. She certainly had not eaten them. Did she have the wrong spot? Impossible! Even hungrier for her exertions, she continues on to her last spot. She is about to start to dig when she notices above her another squirrel. He has frozen in place so as not to be seen, and is obviously looking to hijack her prize. Era thinks quickly and moves ten feet further on and begins to dig there. Obviously finding nothing, she puts on an act of looking disappointed and moves on, noting that she will have to return later when the other squirrel has moved on. Era pauses to consider the situation while hunger and the cold wear on her. She raises her tail above her head as shelter from the falling snow, and decides she will go home. She heads back to her nest and wraps up as warm as she can and waits for the snow to stop.

In the late afternoon Era returns to the feeders. She knows already they have not been filled today, but from watching the birds in previous months had come up with a new idea. Birds are, as she had observed, very messy eaters and seem to drop as many seeds as they eat. So, Era brushed away the snow and searched the ground for anything salvageable. She picked through the husks and the shells hopefully, but alas, there was nothing to eat. She watched jealously as the birds fluttered in and picked at the suet balls. Sadly, beneath this was a tray which caught the bits they dropped, and so, there really was nothing here for her.

Era spent the rest of the day looking for insects to eat,

but sadly none were to be found. She returned to her nest dejected, wrapped herself up as tight as she could and fell asleep both cold and hungry.

Era wakes, and thankfully, the snow is gone. It is, however, cold in the morning light and she is so hungry, she feels pains. Never before has she felt anything like this and she runs to the feeders more in hope than expectation. Today she finds even the suet balls are gone and the birds are in a high state of agitation. She decided to return to her spot from yesterday, confident that the squirrel would at last have moved on; even if he hadn't, she would have to dig and eat for she could not wait any longer.

Thankfully, when she scanned the branches, she saw them empty, and she hurriedly burrowed and rooted around in the earth. A few minutes past and Era scrabbled with increasing desperation. At last she found it and she unearthed the acorn in triumph! It had not even begun to sprout and she raced up the nearest tree with it and quickly consumed it. It has barely made a dent in her hunger, but it felt so good to finally eat something. The rest of the day passed without much event. Era found a few tiny insects to eat and went to sleep as hungry as last night.

The next morning, she awoke in pain and weary, she found getting up harder and had almost no energy whatsoever. She headed to the feeders, and was again disappointed. The anxious birds had grown desperate, and the cacophony of their concern was hard to ignore. Era watched and listened as they flitted about noisily, jealous of their seemingly relentless energy. She decided to stay atop her perch on the feeder and rest, for from here she could scan the garden for any insects or food, which seemed wiser than going to search for it. Hours passed as the birds continued in their noise, and Era watched sadly as they would on occasion catch a worm or a snail.

Her hunger she felt was driving her mad, the instinct and desire to eat was intense. She noted with interest that she did not feel the pain any more, but was just so cold and very tired. She looked for insects as she returned to her tree, but nothing was to be found. She slept early that day and though she woke intermittently; she did not move until the next morning.

Era woke up and blinked at the sun. It was higher in the sky than normal, so she must have overslept. She slowly got up; her senses seemed diminished and the word appeared dull to her. Weak on her feet, she moved shakily along the branch to the trunk and almost without looking descended to the garden. She did not notice the calls of the birds or any difference in her environment as she moved steadily almost by rote towards the feeders. She could tell there was nothing there, however, she climbed up and sat atop one, unsure of what she could do.

She looked at the house nearby, wondering what had happened to the people within that in times before had filled the feeders. She wondered what foods they had within those walls and hungrily imagined giant piles of seeds and almonds and suet balls, of mealworms and acorns and peanuts. She could vividly see the abundance of food and began to hate the people with a jealous intensity. She stood there still in a day dream, in a reverie of seeds and nuts and suet balls, and did not notice the people inside watching her.

She stirred with a start from her trance as the back

door opened and they crossed the garden, with bags of seeds in their arms. Era thought this must be another cruel trick of her mind as they approached her, before scurrying away to a nearby tree. In no time at all they had filled the feeders, and were headed back to the house; Era hungrily cast her eyes about, watching for the cats that often shadowed their footsteps; but she saw nothing as the door closed behind them.

The birds had exploded with celebratory sounds as Era delicately descended from her refuge in the tree and quick as she could, climbed to the feeder. She ate voraciously for some time thinking that she may never be full; until finally, thankfully, she was. She felt her swollen tummy happily and noticed with interest that the people had not closed the lid on the suet balls properly. She saw them watching her from the house, and she eyed them happily as she opened the lid, reached inside and with some difficulty, rolled one up and out of the feeder. It fell and bounced on the floor, thankfully in the direction of her tree. She chased after it and wrestled it up the trunk and along the branch and into her nest. She watched as the people came out and replaced the suet ball and closed the feeder again; their laughter, a delightful sound to Era's ears. She nuzzled up next to her suet ball and happily fell into the deepest of sleeps.

Tanit

(Of Cats)

I wake long before the humans I share my home with. After a large yawn, I stretch out my legs and back and claws, heavily blinking my eyes. I gaze out at my strange housemates, as they lay prone on the bed snoring gently and mumbling strangely in their sleep. I slurp and bite at myself, grooming myself noisily, there's just so much to do and so little time. A quick and violent scratch of my ears, I love the feeling of a nice ear scratch. I close my eyes in pleasure. How do these humans sleep so late? I ponder this most mornings.

I'm hungry now and the food that is in the kitchen for me and my brother will either be stale or most likely, he will have finished it during the night. He normally does, and although he is considerably bigger than me, he knows to stay out of my way. His fur may be thicker and a little longer than mine, but mine is sleeker and glossier. I stand and stretch again on the chair, and I gracefully leap onto the bed. I nuzzle their faces with mine, and I gleefully purr at the sad groaning and moaning from my newly awakened humans. A gentle rub on the tummy, and I flop onto my side and roll over, purring delightedly. A hand slows as he thinks he can just fall back to sleep. I deliver a playful nip to a finger. He moans in surprise before laughing. The time for sleep is over! I meow at him. Feed me! I usher them up and out of bed and run downstairs to await my breakfast.

I sit patiently by my food bowl when the female arrives. As she walks into the kitchen, the dark room is suddenly bathed in light, a wonder I cannot explain but have become accustomed to. For all their awkwardness and clumsiness, they have control of powers that I do not. I eye her suspiciously and with a small degree of envy as she approaches, but then as she lowers her hand and scratches my head, I feel nothing but pleasure. My back arches involuntarily as her hand passes along my spine and then she is stroking my tail. She opens the cupboard, and I see her eyeing food tins and packet. I hope she goes for a tin as they are much better that the packets. "What would you like today, my little Taneee," she coos at me. She brings down a packet, and I try to hide my disappointment. I know what it is already; it's a beef in jelly. She puts it in a dish, and I hear the delightful tinkle of dry food landing in another bowl. I like a mixed breakfast, a combination of wet and dry. She puts the food down, and I sniff it a moment, and then, look up at her. She is watching me expectantly with an expression of great love, and so, I lower my head and dutifully, disappointingly begin to lick all the jelly off the meat. "There's a good girl Tanit," she sings at me and strokes my back while I eat.

The back door opens and I abandon my breakfast and head for the garden, knowing my brother will undoubtedly soon wake and finish off the bowl; he doesn't seem to notice that I only eat the best parts. Outside the morning is in full swing. A light rain pitter-patters on the path and the leaves, and I shiver a bit as the cool wind ruffles my fur. I sniff the air carefully, picking up vague scents of the other cats which have passed through. I grumble to myself about this as I remove their scent marks angrily, a necessary daily ritual. This done, I find myself a nice spot to do my morning business. Soon after I hear the front door open and I run towards it, aware that it is the female human, going off as she does most days for several hours. I have no idea where she goes, or why she goes; only that she does. They're peculiar creatures, but I do love them and I miss them while they're away.

I smell and hear him first! But now, I do see you! I feel my fur stand on end and my tail fluff out to its full size in what must be a terrifying sight to behold. The ginger cat yowls at me and lowers himself to the ground. I slowly and deliberately walk towards the ginger cat that is cowering pathetically before me. I keep moving closer, my shiny black tail reaching straight up behind me. I yowl back at him this time and he sits and stares at me wide eyed, slapping his tail on the ground. I yowl once more, now poised and ready to attack from only a few feet away. I move suddenly, closing the distance immediately, and he flies before me. I give chase eagerly, thundering at his heels. Round and round the house I chase him, before he swerves off another direction, jumps a fence and leaves the garden. I leap after him, landing with a great bang on the fence; here I perch, staring after him malevolently as he disappears into the undergrowth next door.

The front door opens and the male human rushes out

calling my name in a panic. He reaches and picks me up from the fence and gently carries me inside, cooing and murmuring lovingly in my ear. I am still very tense, and can feel adrenaline racing through me as he sets me down in the living room. Then I hear the rattle of treats. Out of nowhere, my brother races into the room and now quickly towards me, sniffing my tail and my face. I push his face away with one paw, and he looks at me scandalised. I stare furiously into his eyes, irritated that he is going to get rewarded for my troubles. My brother is something of a coward, I have to say. He will have a fight with me about once a week, but even though he is such a large cat, he will never chase or fight anything in the garden. He leaves these territory disputes for me, which is very annoying because occasionally I could use his help.

My anger dissipates as treats fall into two bowls. I love treats. They are just so delicious that nothing compares to them! Just the sound of the bag rustling is enough to make me hungry. I hear the male human getting ready to leave for the day, and he now opens the door and waits patiently for us. I go first, calmly strutting out with both my tail and my head raised high. I turn to see my brother, nervously sniffing the air, his feet still inside the house. I shake my head ruefully, finding myself once again doubting that we are actually related. I listen to our human gently encouraging him and watch incredulously as he is literally carried over the threshold. He watches me lazily with his green and somehow amber eyes, completely relaxed and motionless; all the while upside-down in our human's arms. Pathetic, I think as I turn away and go off again into the garden.

I spend much of the day patrolling our territory and honing my skills, terrorising butterflies and insects. I know where Titus is without even checking; deep in the undergrowth, curled up and asleep. There he will remain until our humans return from wherever they go for the best hours of the day. The sun is warm on my black fur, and I begin to feel a bit tired and more than a bit silly. I roll around in some dust and settle myself down in a warm patch of sun on a garden table. Here I pretend to nap, but to all potential threats and prey in the garden, be warned for I am only pretending.

How long have I been asleep? More than an hour for sure, judging by the movement of the sun. I yawn sleepily and notice I am again covered in dust. I spend the next ten minutes grooming and cleaning myself. I think it is important to look my best. Not like my often-dishevelled brother, who sometimes doesn't clean himself enough. I like to look sleek and shiny and deadly. I'm aware I am a pretty cat, as my humans tell me all the time and I cannot see why they would lie. I go off again around the garden, but this time not out in the open and obvious, but through the underbrush stealthily. I watch the birds on the feeders and see that some of them are awfully young. Whereas my brother doesn't often chase or kill birds, he contents himself with clicking at them through a window in some strange parody of their language; I myself am an apex hunter. I lower myself tight to the ground and begin to shuffle stealthily towards the birds. Now that I am close, I wait patiently for the right moment.

For the next hour, I watch carefully as many different families of many different species of birds come to feed barely seven feet away from me. I am waiting for a chick to fly absent-mindedly towards me, or to lose control and spiral low to the ground. It will happen, it always does. I continue my watch as the birds continue to return to the feeder, oblivious to the threat one mere moment away. My eyes narrow as I see a potential victim, a tiny long-tailed tit; dishevelled and barely able to fly it tilts lopsidedly through the air. This will be all too easy, I think to myself. It lands on the feeder and nervously pecks at a fat ball. I almost feel pity for the tiny thing as it scans the world quickly, clueless of the direction from which death is coming. And death is coming. It makes to take flight and teeters pathetically lower and veers towards me. I prepare myself to leap.

I envision slamming my claws into soft flesh! I can actually hear the panicked squeal of terror! I can even taste the creature. As I am about to leap for it, a vole sprints straight past me! Side-tracked, I change my course, but torn between the two, they both somehow get away! As the garden explodes with panicked bird calls, I curse my luck. I grumble to myself while I lower myself to the ground and cross my front paws.

I wake at the sound of a car door slamming. My humans are home! I hear them calling my name (and my brother's) and I arrive at the door as they open it. I stare in bewildered confusion as they fuss over Titus, who is purring loudly as one holds him close. I know a certain big black cat that is going to get jumped on soon, I plot jealously.

While I scheme darkly, I hear food tins being opened and I positively fly back to the kitchen! It's my favourite, a savoury cake of salmon and herring and all other thoughts are forgotten. Now, this truly is delicious! I eat until I feel Titus's giant head forcing me out of my bowl. More than a little irritated, I walk around him and go to his half-eaten bowl of the same salmon and herring and wonder what goes through his mind. Never mind, this is equally delicious.

After feeding, I go to the living room to be adored. After a brush and much attention, I curl up on a sofa pillow and fall asleep. When I wake, Titus is sitting on all fours in front of the television. He looks dejected and sad, so I go down to him. I lick his ear in greeting, and he purrs softly. I begin to groom him, my big soft brother and appreciate how majestic and powerful he actually is. Such beautiful thick fur I muse as I groom him, not too long but longer, much longer than mine. I choose this moment to jump on him. He rolls over and throws me off easily. I lick one of my front paws and eye him carefully. He looks at me darkly for a moment or two, and then with a great sigh, he settles himself back on the floor; he looks much less dejected now. I smile to myself as I return to the sofa. Soft handles tickle my ears, and I find myself purring before I inexorably fall asleep.

Laura

(Of People)

Laura wakes up to the thud of Tanit jumping on the bed. She feels the black cat nuzzle her face and marvels at how soft the cat feels against her skin. The cat purrs delightedly and continues to nuzzle and paw at her. "OK. OK. I'm getting up." Tanit follows her quickly out of the bedroom and waits patiently outside the bathroom door. She dresses and goes downstairs with Tanit at her heels, and finds Titus already waiting by the food bowl. He nuzzles her feet excitedly and she picks him up and cuddles him, he wriggles and writhes eager to be put down and fed. She puts food down for the two cats and watches them. They both seem disappointed with her choice today and she opens the door for them. A soft rain is falling outside and the cats both sit by the door and look out at the world. She sighs and makes breakfast. When she next glances at the door, she sees the cats are gone, and she puts the bowls outside for them before closing the door. Tanit runs up at the sound of the door closing and seeing her on the other side, Laura opens it for her. Tanit eyes her in confusion and sits just outside the door looking in. Laura sighs and reaches down to stroke the cat, wishing she could just stay at home today. Tanit runs inside, away from her touch and she smiles sadly to herself. "I love you too, pudding," she tells Tanit as she brings one of the bowls back inside and closes the door. She gets ready for work and locks the front door behind her; her umbrella up, she walks down the path to the car. As she opens the car door, she pauses and looks about at the garden sprawling around to the front of the house. "Such a peaceful little place," she mutters to herself as she puts her umbrella down and gets in the car, driving away to work.

The End